Illustrated by Art Mawhinney, Animagination, Inc., Liberum Donum Studios,
Michelle Simpson, Maurizio Campidelli, and Meg Roldan

Customer Service: 1-877-277-9441 or customerservice@pikidsmedia.com

Published by Phoenix International Publications, Inc.
8501 West Higgins Road   59 Gloucester Place
Chicago, Illinois 60631   London W1U 8JJ

www.pikidsmedia.com

PI Kids and *we make books come alive* are trademarks of
Phoenix International Publications, Inc., and are registered
in the United States.

Look and Find is a trademark of Phoenix International Publications, Inc.,
and is registered in the United States and Canada.

ISBN: 978-1-5037-5456-0

BEST OF
PIXAR

we make books come alive®
pi kids Phoenix International Publications, Inc.
Chicago • London • New York • Hamburg • Mexico City • Sydney

Pixar movies make us laugh, cry, and think. They answer the important questions like: What do toys really do when we leave the room? What if cars didn't need humans to drive them? And what would our emotions say if they had feelings themselves? These films prove that friendship is powerful, love is greater than fear, and dreams are worth following. And they show us that no matter who (or what) you are, everyone has a story that's worth being told.

MONSTERS, INC.

Sulley and Mike are the top scare team at Monsters, Inc., but humans are just as terrifying to them. When they meet Boo, they realize that humans aren't as scary as they thought, and, in fact, they can be friends. Now the factory harnesses power from laughter, not screams.

TOY STORY

Woody, Buzz, Bo Peep, and friends are always up for adventure, both in Andy's imagination and in real life! When a toy is in trouble, they'll do whatever it takes to save it. From Sid's house to toy stores to daycare to carnivals, these toys are always there for each other and for their kids.

FINDING NEMO / FINDING DORY

Nemo likes adventure. And for Dory, every day is a new adventure—especially because she can't remember what happened yesterday. Marlin isn't a big fan of adventures—they can be dangerous! But when his friends and family need him, he'll swim way outside his comfort zone, rescuing Nemo and helping Dory find her parents, and herself.

THE INCREDIBLES

The Parrs aren't your typical family, but they do pretend to be—most of the time. Whether they're working hard to keep their super identities hidden from the rest of the world or using their powers to stop the bad guys and save the day, this super family isn't just great—they're *incredible*!

CARS

Lightning McQueen is used to living life in the fast lane. But with help from his friends in Radiator Springs, he discovers that there's more to life than coming in first place. From helping friends in trouble to helping train the next generation of racers, Lightning has learned that when you put others before yourself, everyone wins.

RATATOUILLE

Remy has always dreamed of being a chef, but his family doesn't support his dream—and also, he's a rat. But when he ends up in the restaurant of his chef idol, Gusteau, he is finally able to put his skills to work. Together with the garbage-boy-turned-"chef" Linguini, Remy proves Gusteau's motto: "Anyone can cook."

WALL•E

WALL•E is a curious little trash compactor robot who works hard cleaning up the mess that humans have left on Earth. EVE is a probe bot sent to Earth to search for signs of life. Their heartwarming friendship transcends their programming and shows the desensitized humans of the future that the most powerful force is love.

UP

Carl and his wife Ellie had always hoped for adventure, but this trip to Paradise Falls is not the kind Carl planned—not with stowaway Russell, lost tropical bird Kevin, and talking dog Dug messing everything up. When Carl can finally let go of his expectations and the past, he's ready to embrace a new adventure with new friends.

BRAVE

Merida is an independent princess who doesn't want her life to be decided for her. She uses a magic spell to try to make her mother understand—but it isn't a roaring success. Together, mother (who has turned into a bear) and daughter find a way to resolve their differences and mend the bond broken by pride.

INSIDE OUT

Joy is the proud leader of Riley's emotions in Headquarters, guiding Riley through life with perpetual optimism. Per Joy's orders, Sadness tries to keep out of the way. But when Riley's family moves across the country, everything is thrown out of order. Despite their differences, Joy and Sadness manage to join forces to restore emotional balance to Riley's life.

COCO

Miguel has always wanted to be a musician, but his family won't allow it. He disobeys them to follow his dream—and ends up getting cursed instead. As he tries to get back to the Land of the Living, Miguel discovers some secrets that change his family's history, and its future as well.

ONWARD

Ian never got a chance to meet his father. Then, on his 16th birthday, he is given a magic spell to bring his dad back for one day! Unfortunately, the spell goes wrong, and only Dad's bottom half appears. Oops. Ian and his brother Barley set off on a quest to fix the spell, with their half-dad along for the wild ride.

Andy is great at dreaming up adventures for his toys!
When Woody must save Bo Peep from the Evil Dr. Porkcho
Buzz Lightyear comes to lend a hand and help Bo Peep
escape. While they execute their rescue plan, find Buzz and
these other toys that want to help too:

When Andy's toys are donated to Sunnyside Daycare, Lotso assures them that their worries are over. The toys believe it—the Butterfly Room looks like toy heaven! Look around for these other toys that call Sunnyside home:

After Woody and Forky help Gabby Gabby finally find a kid they reunite with the rest of the toys at the carnival. Forky is excited to return to life with Bonnie, and Woody is excited for whatever comes next. While the friends, old and new, hug it out try to find these oblivious humans:

This is the Scare Floor, where monsters are preparing to scare. Everyone is trying to be very frightening, but even monsters need a little help sometimes. Find these things that can help the monsters meet their scare quotas:

Today is Nemo's first day of school. He and his father Marlin meet the teacher, Mr. Ray, at the schoolyard. Right away, Nemo wanders off with some of his new classmates. While Marlin worries about his son, find Nemo, Mr. Ray, and these others who have gathered for the big day:

After traveling across the ocean in search of her parents, Dory finally finds the blue tangs in the aquarium! They tell Dory that her mom and dad escaped to the ocean to wait for her to return home. As Dory takes in this news, see if you can find these other blue tangs that aren't her parents:

Bob would love some alone time, so he convinces Edna Mode to babysit for a little while. It's hard enough to keep track of one Jack-Jack, let alone 50! While Bob and Edna try to get the youngest Incredible's new power under control, help them keep an eye on these Jack-Jacks:

Disney · PIXAR Cars

Wheels-down, Lightning McQueen's favorite place in Radiator Springs is Mater's junkyard. That's where Lightning hangs out with his best buddy, Mater! Today, the friends are having a junkyard scavenger hunt. Help them find these brand-new pieces of junk:

When the World Grand Prix is over, Lightning and his friends return to Radiator Springs. After the adventure they had, it's good to be home. While everyone enjoys the party, find these souvenirs and refreshments:

In the middle of the Florida 500, Lightning decides that Cruz should finish the race. She takes the chance and revs with it. In a classic Doc Hudson maneuver, she flips over Storm to take the lead—and win! While the crowd cheers, scan the stands for these friends and spectators:

WALL·E's job is to clean up Earth. As he makes cubes of garbage, he picks out the most interesting things for himself. But he has his own idea of what's valuable. While he takes a break from his seemingly endless task, find these things he doesn't think are worth keeping:

Mayhem has broken out in the Great Hall! King Fergus is surprised when Merida interrupts and is able to stop the fighting. While Merida's mum stays out of sight, scan the crowd for these speechless clansmen:

Joy and Bing Bong get separated from Sadness and end up in the Memory Dump, where memories disappear. Joy is almost ready to give up...but Bing Bong has a plan! While he and Joy try to escape, find these things that Riley has almost forgotten:

In times of old, the realm was a place of powerful magic, perilous quests, and fearless adventurers! But these days, Ian Lightfoot's greatest trial is avoiding awkward small talk with his neighbors. Look around to find these residents of New Mushroomton going about their everyday lives: